BLUE RABBIT
— AND THE —
RUNAWAY WHEEL

CHRISTOPHER WORMELL

Phyllis Fogelman Books · New York

One day when Blue Rabbit was
looking for adventure instead
of where he was going…

he hit a large rock and the wheel
came off his bicycle.

Blue Rabbit landed with a bump, but he soon got up and went off to look for the lost wheel, which had rolled away down the road.

He had not gone far when he met a squirrel collecting firewood.

"Hello, Squirrel," said Blue Rabbit. "That's a fine pile of firewood you have there."

"Firewood!" said Squirrel angrily. "I was building a little house when —*whizz! crash!*—I turned around to find I had only a pile of broken sticks."

"Oh, dear," said Blue Rabbit. "I wonder what that whizzing was."

"I don't know, but whatever the whizz was, it went that way," said Squirrel, pointing down the road. "And I'm going after it."

Down the road they met Badger sitting in a muddy puddle.

"Hello, Badger," said Blue Rabbit. "Nice day for a mud bath."

"Is it?" said Badger grumpily. "I was just thinking what a nice day it was *not* to take a mud bath, especially in this very unpleasant puddle. Then—*bump! splash!*—I was taking one."

"**P**robably the whizzing thing bumped into you," suggested Squirrel.

"Whatever it was, it must have been on a bike," said Badger, pointing to the muddy track of a bicycle wheel. "And I'm going to follow it."

"On a bike," said Blue Rabbit to himself. "Oh, dear."

Farther down the road they met a tortoise lying on his back.

"Hello, Tortoise," said Squirrel and Badger.

Blue Rabbit said, "It's a nice day for sunbathing."

"Sunbathing, am I?" said Tortoise. "I thought the world was ending. *Whoosh! Bang!* Suddenly everything turned upside down and spun around.… Would you mind turning me over, please? Thanks a lot."

"It must have been the whizzing thing," said Squirrel.

"On a bike," added Badger.

"It may *not* have been," said Blue Rabbit hopefully. "It may have been an earthquake."

"Earthquakes don't ride bikes," said Badger, pointing to the muddy wheel track. "Come on, if we follow the track, we're bound to catch the culprit sooner or later."

And they did.
For as they followed the track of the whizzing wheel, it took them in a wide, wide circle that led right back to the very rock where Blue Rabbit had crashed. And there it stopped.

"Why, there's my bike!" exclaimed Blue Rabbit.

"Your bike?" said Squirrel and Tortoise.

"Then that muddy wheel must belong to *your* bike!" said Badger.

"Well, I guess it does," said Blue Rabbit, putting the wheel back on. "You see, it fell off and rolled away and . . . um . . . " He stopped, for Squirrel, Badger, and Tortoise were looking very upset.

"So *you're* the Reckless Rider," they cried angrily.

But before they could catch him, the Reckless Rider hopped on his bike and was off down the road, leaving only the track of a muddy bicycle wheel behind him.

For Eliza

First published in the United States 2001
by Phyllis Fogelman Books
An imprint of Penguin Putnam Books for Young Readers
345 Hudson Street • New York, New York 10014
First published in the United Kingdom 1999 by
Jonathan Cape Ltd, Random House
Copyright © 1999 by Christopher Wormell
All rights reserved
Printed in Hong Kong
1 3 5 7 9 10 8 6 4 2

Library of Congress Cataloging-in-Publication Data available upon request

The art for this book was prepared using lino block printing.